Stress Relief

Her First Woman – Series 1

Steph Brothers

Contents

Blurb

She's tired of working her fingers to the bone...

Bryony has midterm exams in less than a week, and is surviving on nothing but coffee, tension, and the abject fear of failure. She knows she needs a break—and maybe a mind-blowing orgasm or two—but can't tear herself away from the books.

But when she loses her mind at Payton, her friend and housemate, Bryony finally realizes she's gone right off the deep end.

As a personal trainer with life experience, Payton knows that what her younger friend needs is just some down time. A little breathing space, a stretch or two, and some quiet meditation.

But when she soothes Bryony's tortured brow, and eases her tension, a whole different connection opens up between them. One that goes into brand new territory for Bryony.

Find Me Here

Free TABOO e-book for newsletter signup!

Come and read more of my work on Medium!

Or come and ogle my tweets?

Ooh, and I'm on the Facebooks as well!

Stress Relief

I sat at my desk, staring at the text book open in front of me. Each of those words made perfect sense. But in that moment, only a week before midterms, they all ganged up on me, blurring together until they looked like nothing but a wall of gibberish.

I'd been studying for 9 hours now, with five minute breaks for cups of coffee or calls of nature. And the more I had of the first, the more I needed of the second.

In desperation, I sat back on my chair and stared at the ceiling, trying a pep talk on myself.

"Come on, Bryony. You *know* this stuff."

I tried to think of what my housemate would do. Payton was a few years older than me, and worked as a personal trainer. She never seemed to get stressed at all. What advice had she given me before? Breathing. I think she said that was a useful thing to do.

With a few long, cleansing breaths, I felt calm enough to tackle the books again. Right up until I looked at the words and they all turned back into hazy ants.

There was a tiny rational part of my brain which screamed at me to take a proper break. To relax and refresh, and let my mind wander.

The trouble was, that tiny part was stuck deep down inside, surrounded by stressed-out-monkey-in-the-jungle parts, all of which were screaming at me to learn more, to cram more, to just be smarter at this stuff.

With no better ideas, I figured it was time to make yet another coffee. If caffeine couldn't fix this problem, then nothing could.

Okay, so maybe a good, hard, anonymous fuck would help, but who had time to go fishing for cock? I sure didn't.

No, I needed some kind of friends-with-benefits gig. That would be perfect right now. But ever since I arrived in LA from good ol' Worland, Wyoming, I'd been emotionally celibate.

Don't get me wrong, I'd ridden my share of stallions—and ponies, unfortunately—in the past two years. I'd just made sure never to let a guy mess with my situation. With my body, sure, but never with my mind.

Now was definitely not the time to be breaking in a new ride, in any case. I needed someone who could read my fucking mind and simply get me off in three minutes flat. Maybe rub my feet for a while afterward. Was that *really* too much to expect?

I couldn't even ask Payton for a spare dude, either. She didn't swing that way. In fact, one of the main reasons I was so happy living here was because she only ever brought girls home. I could deal with feminine madness any day of the week. It was masculine chaos that was sure to kill my study time.

Giving up on the idea of orgasm therapy for the moment, I marched out to the kitchen and switched on the electric kettle. I fished a cup off the rack and set it up, ready to go. But when I opened the coffee tin, I almost collapsed.

"Payton!"

My housemate came sauntering casually into the kitchen, still dressed in her skin-tight workout clothes. "What's up, Bry?"

I shoved the open—and empty—coffee tin almost into her face. "What is the meaning of this?"

Payton used her superior height and strength to push the tin away. "It's empty. I used the last of it when I got home."

"But I need it! What the hell were you thinking?"

"Uh, that I needed a cup of coffee. You know it was nearly half-full when I left this morning, right?"

I slammed the tin down onto the floor of the kitchen and pointed my finger into her face. The monster of stress had my head in his jaws and wasn't letting go.

"Well, screw you anyway. I have to study."

And with that, I turned on my heel and marched back to my room, making sure to scream as I slammed my door.

God, I hated myself at that moment, but it felt as if my whole life was out of control. I sat on the corner of my bed and put my head in my hands. Rocking forward and back seemed somehow to help. The tears that were running down my cheeks did nothing for me, though.

Poor Payton. She didn't deserve any of that. I just hoped she wouldn't hold it against me.

I was destined to get my answer sooner than I hoped, as I heard her footsteps approaching my door. She didn't knock, simply flinging it open and stepping inside, her hands on her hips.

Before she could even say a word, I ran to her and threw my arms around her neck. "I'm so sorry, Payton. I'm such a bitch. I didn't mean it."

Thankfully she just stood firm, and put her arms around me, resting her hands on my back. "Shh. It's okay, honey."

For some reason, I felt my stress easing a little. Not much, but enough that I could get my tears back under control. Maybe it was because she was older, and maybe it was because with her height advantage I found my head resting on her chest. Whatever the reason, she was more like a big sister to me at that moment than a housemate. Maybe even a little like a mom.

"I'm just so stressed out with exams coming."

"I get it. And I'm actually in awe of you."

"Y–you are?"

Payton ran her hands up and down my back, letting her nails dig through the fabric just enough to really bring my skin to life. "Why do you think I quit college in my first year? I couldn't handle that kind of stress."

"I don't have the same kind of wisdom you do. Or people skills, clearly. I need this degree or I'll have no career." My tears came rushing out again, even faster than before, and Payton squeezed me a little harder.

"Come on. You're gonna be fine. But you definitely need to take a break, honey."

She pushed me back and sat me down on the bed, then rested her hands on my shoulders. I put my hands on hers and sighed. "Thanks, Payton. I'm usually not this mental."

"Bry, you're exactly this mental every time exams come around."

"Then you definitely shouldn't have taken the last of the coffee!"

She squeezed my shoulders again and brought her hands up to cup my cheeks. Kneeling before me she dried my tears with her thumbs and smiled. "You crazy kid. I'd say something about you burning the candle at both ends, but I don't think your other end has had anything hot near it for months."

I couldn't stop the heat rising in my cheeks. I knew Payton was fooling with me, but somehow it felt like I should be embarrassed. As if I was somehow undesirable.

Payton came up to sit beside me on the bed, putting her arm around me in a sisterly way. "You probably just need some sleep, Bry."

"Maybe. But I'm so keyed up. I know myself well enough to know I'll never sleep when I'm like this." I put my hands together on top of my knees, feeling like a schoolgirl about to ask the principal for a hall pass.

"Do you have, like...any Valium? Or just something to take the edge off for me?"

"Sorry, honey. I'm a personal trainer. I stay away from all of that stuff." She brushed my hair back from my forehead. "I could recommend some physical remedies. If you're interested."

Was she offering what I thought she was offering? The idea of getting hot and heavy with a woman was...well, actually, it was kinda hot.

Wait. What the fuck? I'm straight.

"Oh, um...are you sure? I mean, don't you have a...a girl-friend?"

I'd blushed at the thought she was hitting on me. I was even more embarrassed when she started laughing.

"Oh, Bry, I'm sorry. I don't mean to make you shy. I was actually talking about some stretches and meditative tech-niques."

"Ha. Okay. Sorry, of course you were."

"Interesting, though."

"Wh–what?"

Payton reached across and tapped my nose with her finger.

"That you didn't say no. Or call me crazy."

"Umm..."

"And *my* answer is no, by the way. I *don't* have a girlfriend."

I knew I was straight. Sure, I'd watched my share of hot girl-on-girl porn. Maybe more than my share. Sometimes that's what it took for me to get myself off. Fantasies are damn fun. But to actually do it? Like, in real life? That would be...

"Bry? You still with me?"

"Yes, I think so." I put my hands on my cheeks. The heat in them suddenly wasn't from embarrassment. Shyness, maybe. But most of it was a sudden burst of arousal.

"Bry? Honey, did you...did you *want* me to?"

"Um. I d–don't know."

Payton slid down on to her knees again. "Honey, sex can be an amazing reset button, for sure. And you know I think you're the sweetest, cutest young thing going around."

"Thanks." That was true. She'd told me plenty of times how hot I was.

"Bry, I could rock your world if you'd let me, and it would be my fucking pleasure to do it." She lifted my hands and kissed them. "But you would have to relax and let me."

The thought of Payton touching me intimately, in the way that only *boys* had ever done, filled my brain with fuzz. It robbed me of the power to think for the moment.

All I knew was the blood was rushing through my body so fast I could barely hear, and my breath was racing to keep up.

And holy fucking hell, my pussy was so wet I thought my jeans and panties might just slide off of their own accord.

It took me a few seconds to find my voice again. "I–I just need to be clear, though, Pay. I really don't think I could...um...do much. Y'know, in return."

"Shh. It's okay. This is not about that."

Without another word, Payton moved her lithe body up onto the bed behind me and slid those long, slender legs around mine. Like she was a cocoon for me. "I tell you what, Bry. Let's not make any decisions right now. How about we start out with just a little bit of what I actually meant?"

"Okay." My voice was tiny, even to my own ears.

"And if it should happen to feel right, we can move on to what you *thought* I meant. Deal?"

"Uh huh..." The truth was, just having another human being wrapped up tight against me was already easing some of my stress. Her warmth toasted my skin, and every time she spoke, her words floated into my ears like aural hot chocolate.

Payton slipped her hands around in front of me and worked at the buttons on my blouse. I stiffened my spine automatically, but I managed to stop my hands from gripping hers. When she'd opened the garment up I let her slide it off me.

"It works much better with skin to skin contact." Her voice was so low it was almost a hum, and it had a wonderful calming effect. But when she moved her hands down to the button of my jeans I tensed up again.

"A-are you sure about that?"

"It's up to you. But whether I use my powers for good or evil, *wink-wink*, it's still much better with nothing between us."

"Y-you mean... you'll be... as well?"

"Of course, honey. Wouldn't you feel more relaxed if I was naked too?"

I swallowed heavily with my eyes closed, and simply nodded. God, that sounded hot and perfect. Nothing between us. Just her beautiful, smooth, feminine skin against mine. I had to squeeze my legs together to try and ease the wanton tingling between them.

Payton smiled and moved back away from me a little. "Then maybe you'd be more comfortable if you take care of your clothes, and I'll take care of mine."

I stood and glanced in Payton's direction but made no move to strip any further. It wasn't just shyness on my part. I'd seen her in her skin-tight workout wear and she was a damn goddess. Tall and slender, with perfect muscle tone and some gorgeous shape about her.

It didn't matter at that moment that this was supposed to be about relaxation. I was simply hoping my pale skin and rounded flesh didn't turn her off.

Finally, I turned my back to her and eased the rest of my clothes off. It just seemed easier to let her see my bare ass before anything else.

"Turn around, honey. Please?"

I slowly did as she asked, struggling to meet her eyes. That was *all* down to shyness. It was pretty damn confronting to suddenly be naked in front of my housemate.

"Oh, god. You're so fucking gorgeous, Bry."

Her praise was like some weird and wonderful voodoo. I was suddenly a goddess. With my big boobs and my soft belly, my rounded hips and natural bush. I chanced a look at Payton and as perfect as she looked in workout gear, she was even more amazing naked. Everything in proportion and so tight and tanned. And hairless. We were pretty close to opposites.

She leaned over and patted my bed. "Lie down here, honey. On your front."

I did as she said, holding my breath as I waited for the next step. Wondering how I'd cope if she went rogue like a guy would and started poking at me in places I wasn't ready to be poked.

I shouldn't have worried.

I felt her weight settle above me, one leg either side of my hips. There was an unmistakable heat radiating from between her thighs, down over the sensitive skin of my ass, but there was almost no contact down there. Simply her inner thighs right against the widest part of my hips.

The first touch came from her hands, and it was in my hair, not on my skin. She scooped up my russet brown locks and pulled on them, softly and gently, awakening a wonderful sensation in my scalp.

"You are such a beautiful girl, Bryony. It hurts me sometimes that you won't enjoy it. Treat yourself nicely. Or even just *decently.*"

"Uhh..."

"Sometimes I think...it's as if you're punishing yourself for having such an excellent brain. You don't want to admit you have a fucking amazing bod as well."

She trailed her fingers through my hair, and then kept on moving down my back to my waist. The skin on my butt cheeks tingled in anticipation of her touch, but the teasing wench moved back up again, scratching my back deeply like she had before, only without the fabric to block her this time.

"God, you have amazing hands, Pay."

"You think this is good? You should see what...no, sorry. I shouldn't, um..."

"What? Payton, what?"

When she spoke again, there was a little rasp in her voice, and she sounded embarrassed. "I was going to say things that...well, I was probably rushing the situation."

I closed my eyes and held my breath a moment. Then made a decision. "Say it? Please?" The moment the words came out, I realized I'd committed myself—in my own head, at least—to whatever could, or would, happen. All the possibilities seemed...*workable.*

"I was going to say you should see what else I can do with them. My hands, I mean."

The breath that came from me then was shaken by the tremors running through my entire body. I swallowed hard and spoke before I could change my mind. "Show me?"

"You sure, honey?"

"Hell, no. But please...do it anyway?"

"Ohh. My pleasure." She pressed her hand to the center of my back. "And yours, too. I promise."

Payton rested her body on top of mine, the hard points of her nipples poking into my shoulder blades. She scooped my hair aside and kissed my neck, gliding up until she could sink her teeth into my ear lobe. It's like she knew every single weak point on my body, though that wasn't really a stretch. They were probably the same ones she had.

She glided sideways off me and clawed her hand around my hip. I took the hint and rolled onto my back. Payton's eyes zeroed in on my breasts, and the aftershocks my movement had given them.

"Fuck, you're gorgeous, honey."

"Thank you."

She leaned down and pressed her lips to mine, softly, like she was scared I'd run. There was a huge burst of adrenaline coursing through me, for sure, but it was nothing to do with fight, fright or flight. It was a whole other f-word causing it.

I parted my lips and let Payton dance her tongue between them. The taste of her mouth was almost sweet, or maybe it was just the softness. I was so used to stubble and force, and she was all smoothness and grace. It was like she was teasing my tongue across the divide and into her mouth. And damn, the girl was an amazing kisser.

As our mouths grew wider and our tongues delved deeper, Payton brought her hands up to my neck, caressing it either side and bending my head to wherever she needed it.

I couldn't contain the sweet sigh that flowed out of me. The way she'd wordlessly coaxed me into giving over control like that was a huge step toward relaxation.

I dared not pull my hands up off the bed, for fear I'd mess things up. I didn't really want to do very much. If I could simply touch her skin, I'd be happy. My worry was that with my inexperience, I'd go too far, too soon.

Having only been with guys before, that was the dynamic I understood. *Do everything, right now.* But the way Payton was nuzzling at my throat with that pretty mouth of hers had me all confused. In the most beautiful and illicit way.

She laid a trail of heated kisses down one side of my neck and up the other. When she reached my ear, she bit lightly into the lobe and then murmured to me in that hot chocolate voice of hers. "You feeling more relaxed now, honey?"

"Uh-huh…"

"Wait until I give you the works."

"Ohh…"

Payton raised herself, kneeling above me and gazing into my eyes. She reached out and placed the pointer finger of each hand together on my lips, like she was telling me not to speak. With a sexy little smile on her own face she ran those fingers down the center of my body, between my breasts and on to my belly. The lower she took them, the wider she spread her arms, until she came to rest with one hand on each of my hips.

Payton rested her weight on me as she lifted her leg. Before I registered what was happening, my sexy housemate had one knee pressing between my tightly clamped thighs.

Gradually I let her push my legs apart, and I bit my lip as the cool air kissed the hot slickness of my pussy. For some reason, my entire body trembled. I knew I wasn't cold, and I didn't think I was scared. Not *super*-scared, at least.

But the look on Payton's face, and the soft but strong way she was guiding me into the experience, had my belly clamping with want.

Now kneeling between my thighs, Payton fell forward until her nose was touching mine. "Are you ready?"

"Yes. Please."

She kissed me again, just a soft touch of lips on lips, before drifting slowly south. Payton glided her soft, slender body over me, as well as her mouth. She picked up my hands and threaded our fingers together, pushing until my arms were up beside my head.

Softly, Payton slid her face all over my breasts, letting the silky skin of her cheek and lips tickle over every inch of them. Only when she'd explored them completely did she open up and pull one stiff bud into her mouth.

When she closed around my nipple, she was so soft about it I almost begged her to bite. It was the most delicious torture. The heat of her lips and tongue were almost perfect, but I needed her to do more. Suck that tender flesh. Bite it. Run her stiff tongue in circles.

I didn't remember speaking, and was convinced all I'd done was moan with pleasure. Somehow, though, Payton understood exactly what I needed.

She drew harder on my nipple, awakening sweet tingles of pleasure all through that sensitive flesh, and beneath it. If I could have freed my hands I would have cupped my full breasts and presented them to her. Dared her to go for broke.

As it was, though, she was setting the pace...and she was just so fucking patient. If she kept teasing like this, all my relaxation would turn to frustration.

Holy hell. When did I turn into such a slut? I mean, she'd barely started touching me before I let her talk me into sex. Or did I talk her into it?

But while I was being honest with myself, no matter which of us drove it, this had happened far more easily than it *ever* had with a guy.

As Payton switched across to my other nipple, she relaxed her grip on my hands, scratching light trails with her fingers, inward on my arms. The moment she pressed my tits together she brought her knee forward to kiss my pussy, and I pulled in a whispered breath of surprise. It was pretty close to overwhelming, but bizarrely, it was still nowhere near enough. I closed my eyes for fear of being completely overloaded.

With a sweet wet sound, Payton released my stiff bud and moved down to my belly. "God, you're cute, Bry."

I couldn't think of anything to say to that. Thanking her didn't seem right, especially since I already had. Truth was, I'd wanted a body like hers for as long as I could remember, so to have her worshipping mine was a strange and wonderful delight.

"Oh, baby..." Her voice had turned syrupy and soft. "You smell so sweet."

My eyes flew open of their own accord. "Wait...you mean...down there?"

"Uh huh." She licked at the skin on my hip, and my breath shuddered as quakes of need ran through me. "I hope you don't mind, but I'm going to have to eat your gorgeous little pussy now."

She hoped I didn't *mind?* Was she on drugs? I could feel my mouth searching for the right shape to make some kind of words, but before they could finish the job Payton stole every thought from my mind.

She glided the tip of her hot tongue up the length of my slit, pressing harder when she reached the peak. I struggled to find my next breath as she made a circle around my clit.

And though I'd managed to keep some kind of control over my voice throughout, that was my breaking point. At first it was just a breath coursing out of me, but before it finished, I was moaning like the wanton little hussy I was.

My housemate suddenly stopped, drawing her tongue back into her mouth and moaning. "Mm. You taste fucking awesome, Bry."

"Um...th–thank you."

Before I could speak again, Payton clawed her hands around my thighs and drove her hot, glistening tongue against my slick lips. I barely knew what I was doing as shock after shock of pleasure fired through me.

Every stroke of her delicious tongue fired off new bursts of lightning inside my pussy. Streaks that grew and spread, like jagged vines of bliss climbing through my belly to seize my chest and squeeze it.

I could virtually feel the stress being pushed out through my pores, as Payton's incredible skill filled me with ecstasy instead.

It was as if she'd bewitched me, taking control of my limbs. I seized her hair in one hand and held on, pulling her harder against my crazed little cunt. When that still didn't feel intense enough, I slid my foot around the back of her head and pressed. It was a wonder Payton could even breathe down there.

But she seemed to manage just fine. She sucked and lapped at me like a crazed beast, and I bucked and shuddered with every touch. It was as if she'd somehow mapped out my most intensely sensitive spots and was hitting them, one after the other. Time and time again.

Then, when she drove two fingers deep inside me while she bit at my little detonator, I knew I was gone. It was a done deal. I was about to climax, and for sure it was going to be seismic. Like nothing I'd ever felt before, either with a man or by myself.

I grasped my own boob and squeezed, my thumb and finger forming a pincer around my nipple and tweaking it like hell.

For a brief moment, my senses exploded, leaping outside of my body. Then, like a stretched rubber band, they all fired back into me at the speed of sound, prickling at my skin as they passed through it.

Blow after blow of sheer bliss pounded me, in the chest, in the back, and deep in my belly. Payton growled like a leopard between my thighs, as she rode my bucking body all the way home.

My housemate slowly climbed up toward my mouth, licking and sucking at different patches of my skin as she passed them. I let out a little girly squeal as she nipped at my belly, and then I collapsed on the bed like a big, wet noodle.

She still had her fingers inside me, and she curled them up to push at my special spot inside, just as she bit into my nipple. The mix of sensations electrified me, and I threw my arms around Payton's back.

Slowly, she eased herself up until we were once again face to face. I kinked my head up and took her sweet mouth in a tasty kiss, rich with my own arousal.

Payton parted her soft lips, caressing mine with the same skill and care she'd taken with my other lips. I suddenly felt braver than ever, and crept my hand down her beautifully-toned back. When I reached her tight, round ass, I grasped it like a grapefruit.

"Mmm..." she hummed, straight into my mouth before breaking our kiss. "You don't have to do anything, Bry. I told you that at the start."

"I know. But what if I want to?"

She bit her lip as if to hide the beautiful smile that broke out on her face. "Then who am I to say no?"

I smiled back and gave her ass another, harder, squeeze. Payton closed her eyes, a look of pure desire crossing her beautiful face.

Unsure quite where to go from there, I slid my body a little lower on the bed, and found my face level with her gorgeous boobs. I blew a cool breath over her perky nipple, and giggled like a schoolboy when her skin tightened.

"God, you're so fucking cute, Bry."

Cute was okay, but I wanted to be sexy. So I seized her breast and flicked her stiff bud with my tongue. Payton gasped in reaction, and lowered herself toward me.

I took the hint and drew her nipple into my mouth, suckling on her sweet flesh. She moaned deeply, and the sound vibrated through her skin and into my lips.

"Bite it, honey."

Payton's voice had gone dark with passion, and I couldn't resist her. I did exactly as she asked, securing that stiff little bud between my teeth and squeezing.

She lowered herself onto me, though I couldn't be sure she didn't simply collapse. I snaked my other hand down onto her ass as well, and gripped both of her heavenly cheeks, as tight as I could.

Payton's breath washed over the top of my head, her body weight pressing down on me heavily enough to make breathing difficult. Which was just perfect.

I slid my fingers inward, finding the dark places between her pretty ass cheeks. The instant I touched her drenched pussy lips, she cried out in pleasure.

"Bry..."

That was all she said, and it was more of a whisper than a word. But suddenly, I was not just sexy...I was a goddess.

I pulled my other hand around below her and glided over the beautiful smooth skin of her mound. Remembering how she'd hit all my best places at one time, I figured I'd try the same thing.

I hovered my finger just below her clit as I drew my other hand up to her ass. The world froze for a second, as I blew a cool breath across Payton's sweet nipple.

In a single instant, I wolfed her bud into my mouth as I ground her clit and ass with my fingers. Payton gulped air as she raised her head, eyes closed and mouth gaping.

The thrill of touching another woman so intimately sent my belly buzzing again. Seeing how deeply my touch affected her was even better. But it still wasn't enough. I wanted everything.

I released her nipple and rolled myself to the side, forcing Payton to come off me. She landed on the bed and I clambered on top of her, capturing her wrists in my hands.

My housemate was fitter and stronger, but I had the weight advantage. She tried to wrestle out of my grip, and honestly,

I'm sure she could have if she'd wanted to. Clearly, she had no desire to stop me. And that was just fine.

I hovered above her for a moment, my breath mingling with hers as I gazed into her. She narrowed her eyes and poked her tongue out, flicking my lips with it.

That was enough of a trigger for me, and I fell on her like she'd done with me. I embraced her lips with mine, suckling on her tongue like it was food. Almost automatically, I circled my hips, grinding my pelvic bone into the juicy wetness of her pussy.

The freshness of her scent came up to meet me, mingling beautifully with mine. It was like a sunrise at the beach, and I knew I simply had to dive in. To swim in her, to surf the ripples and waves of her pussy until we were both done.

I released our kiss and nibbled my way down her chin and onto the softness of her throat. Payton hummed lightly, as I licked and sucked at her, finding my way to her breasts and biting her pretty nipples, harder than I had before.

But her sweet and spicy aroma called to me, clearer than ever, and my mouth watered in anticipation. I just hoped I could make her feel even half as good as she did to me.

Finally, I was there, my wet tongue on her silken mound. I looked up, finding her beautiful eyes and holding contact. I needed to see her...to watch what my mouth would do to her.

I glided past her hood, feeling as if I'd dived over a cliff. Payton widened her eyes, as if she'd never believed I'd get there. And for some reason, it really didn't feel weird to be between her thighs, my mouth only a fraction of an inch from her tempting cunt.

I flicked my tongue out, like a snake striking, glancing across her slick lips. Payton blinked and gasped, and that was all the encouragement I needed.

The tiny sample of her flavor burst against the tip of my tongue, and I knew instantly I wanted more. I wanted all of her. I needed to discover every way she could taste.

As I dived into her, I couldn't contain the whimpering moan that coursed out of me. Her lips were soft and wet, and so damn hot. Her texture and her taste filled my senses, and as I lapped away, she bucked and jerked and moaned so beautifully.

"Fuck, Bry...you sure you've never done this?"

"Mm-hmm." I wasn't taking my mouth off her sweet pussy for anything as useless as talking. Not when I could stay there, tongue buried deep inside her, with her velvet thighs as ear-muffs.

Oh, god...my own belly tingled with desire as I thought about what were actually doing. What I was doing. I squeezed my thighs together, but that was never going to be enough.

As I glided my thumb up the sopping wet face of Payton's pussy, I burrowed my other hand down beneath my hips. I found my clit at the same moment I pressed hers, and we cried out in some weird kind of dissonant harmony.

My sexy housemate writhed beneath my touch, and I was truly a goddess at that moment. I'd always been able to make boys moan, but until that moment I'd never believed I could do the same to women.

Payton reached down and took a hold of my hair, pulling my head sideways, and forward, and wherever she needed me. I ground my clit as hard as I could while I soaked up the gorgeous sensation of pleasing another woman.

I lapped and sucked at Payton, and she pulled her thighs together, clamping my head between them. It felt like she must have hooked her ankles around each other as she dug her heels into my lower back and ground her cunt into my mouth.

With all that wonderful toned strength, she forced me to the side, and rolled me onto my back. I simply sighed with desire as she sat heavily on my mouth and pumped herself forward and back over my tongue.

I ground my clit into a frenzy as I squeezed her perfect ass with my other hand. I couldn't get enough of her spicy flavor, as she coated my mouth and chin with all her wonderful juices.

Looking up at Payton, I was in awe of her tight abs, her perky tits, the pink color that had filled her chest, her throat and her cheeks. She was a picture of healthy, horny womanhood, and I kinda fell a little bit in love with her at that moment. Or at least, I was crushing on her as hard as she was crushing on my tongue.

She screwed her mouth up into a snarl as she snatched my hair in her fists. As she pulled my face into her cunt, she circled her hips, and I got my wish. I could taste every part of her desire, and it was all fucking perfect.

And even though she was completely dominating me, it never made me feel weak, or submissive. It was the most perfectly balanced I'd ever been while fucking. It was a totally shared moment.

Especially when she tightened her body, curling downward, clearly in the beginning stages of a climax. Just as I was.

She rode my mouth hard, and I pummeled my clit, and suddenly it was like a dam had burst. Payton howled out her pleasure at the walls and ceiling, and I poured out my climax into the heated wet heart of her perfect cunt.

Payton strained above me, her muscles clamping and releasing as her orgasm seized control of her. She hauled on my hair, and pressed herself down on me.

Finally, the last heaving breath of climax hissed from her throat, and she fell forward, rolling to the side as she landed.

I came up off my belly and dived into her waiting embrace, and she took my mouth in a deep kiss that started out hungry, then grew softer and sweeter the longer we held it.

Finally, I pulled away and peppered her cheek with little pecks, until I collapsed in her arms. I was utterly spent, completely satisfied...and for the moment at least, stress-free.

"Thank you so much, Payton."

"Ah, honey. Thank *you*. That was...you were *so fucking good*."

"You sound surprised."

"I am, honey. I thought you were straight."

"So did I."

She ran her short-nailed fingers down my back, awakening little tingles of pleasure. "So, you feeling a little more relaxed, now?"

"Absolutely." Out of nowhere, an enormous yawn took over me. I'd been depriving myself of so much sleep, just to get ready for exams. Suddenly, it all caught up with me.

Payton slid me down onto my back, and pulled herself right up beside me. She put one arm and one leg across my body, and kissed me on the forehead.

"You sleep now, honey. The books won't miss you."

The thickness of slumber was already filling my head. As I drifted lower, my senses drew in everything about my beautiful bed-partner. The scent of her hair, the feel of her skin.

And most of all, the taste of her perfect pussy.

The greatest stress relief of all time.

THE END

Preview of She's The Boss

Clara's boss Margot has been riding her hard for months now. Finding fault, correcting her, just being a complete bitch.

But things come to a head during a private meeting. When Clara announces she's quitting, Margot's attitude changes...and she reveals the plans she's had all along for the beautiful young employee.

Hint...they're dirty.

AVAILABLE ON AMAZON AND KINDLE UNLIMITED!

About The Author

Steph Brothers likes it dirty and writes it that way. Stories with claws to scratch all your deepest, darkest and naughtiest itches.

Also By Steph Brothers

• KISS HER BETTER

• SHARE & SHARE ALIKE

• HOLLYWOOD SEX SCENE

OR GRAB MY BOX SET!
QUICK, SLICK & LONGING TO LICK

• MY MASSEUSE

• DERBY DOMINATION

• THE COPY ROOM

• BAD BRIDE-TO-BE

• MY GIRL CRUSH

• MY PUNISHMENT

OR GRAB MY BOX SET!

OR GET ALL THOSE GIRLS TOGETHER IN *MY BIG, WET BOX SET!*

MORE GIRL-ON-GIRL

WORKING WOMEN
ASSERTIVENESS TRAINING

• SPOILT   • STRAPPED   • SATED

OR GRAB MY BOX SET!
LOVERS IN LAW

• DON'T GET CAUGHT • DON'T GET HITCHED

• DON'T LET HER GO • DON'T LOOK BACK

OR GRAB MY BOX SET!

FFM

• SINGLE BELLES, SINGLE BELLES
OLDER MAN, YOUNGER WOMAN EROTICA
ROUGH & RISKY (Multi-author series)

• IN THE CLASSROOM

• ON THE INTERSTATE

• IN THE OUTFIELD

• IN THE TOOLSHED

• ON HIS YACHT

OR GRAB ALL FIVE AT ONCE – IN THE BOX!

THE A–Z OF AGE GAP EROTICA

• ALLISON • BETHANY • CASSIE • DESTINY • EMILY

OR GRAB THE A–E BOX SET!

• FABIENNE • GIA • HALLIE • ISIS • JAZLYN

OR GRAB THE F–J BOX SET!

HOTWIFE EROTICA

FIXING MY HUSBAND'S HOT MESS SERIES

• TAKEN BY MY HUSBAND'S BOSS

• HIS BOSS'S ESCORT

• PAYING HIS DEBT

• SUBMITTING TO MY HUSBAND'S BOSS

• REWARDING MY HUSBAND'S BODYGUARD

• WON BY MY HUSBAND'S BROTHER

OR GRAB MY BOX SET!
BULL MARKET (BMWW)

• YVETTE GETS WET TO PAY HER MAN'S DEBT

• JILL GETS HER FILL TO PAY HER MAN'S BILLS

• JEWEL GETS THE TOOL 'CAUSE HER MAN IS A FOOL

• VICKY GETS SLICK JUST TO KICK HER MAN'S TICKET

• BRIGITTE GETS THE MEAT JUST TO KEEP OFF THE STREETS

• JETTE GETS TO SWEAT 'CAUSE HER MAN LOST HIS BETS

OR GRAB MY BOX SET!

OLDER WOMAN, YOUNGER MAN EROTICA
SILVER BELLES

- BOY, YOU MUST BE A LIBRARY BOOK 'CAUSE I'M CHECKING YOU OUT

- HERE I AM, BOY; SO WHAT ARE YOUR OTHER TWO WISHES?

- LET'S GET ME OUT OF THESE WET CLOTHES

- BOY, YOU MUST BE MY HOMEWORK 'CAUSE I SHOULD BE DOIN' YOU

OR GRAB MY BOX SET!

Made in the USA
Monee, IL
17 September 2023

42906505R00021